TO:

FROM:

For Mrs. Schipfer, who helped me walk through
worry and see the good things ahead.
—EG

For Richard and Rupert, for always.
—SM

Published by Sourcebooks Wonderland, an imprint of Sourcebooks Kids
P.O. Box 4410, Naperville, Illinois 60567–4410
(630) 961-3900
sourcebookskids.com

Cataloging-in-Publication Data is on file with the Library of Congress.

Source of Production: Phoenix Color, Hagerstown, Maryland, United States of America
Date of Production: April 2022
Run Number: 5024181

Printed and bound in the United States of America.
PHC 10 9 8 7 6 5 4 3 2 1

Little Yellow Bus

words by Erin Guendelsberger
pictures by Suzie Mason

sourcebooks
wonderland

The little yellow bus woke up to a morning that was clear and bright. Outside the garage window, birds were singing their sunrise songs. From down the street came smells of delicious breakfast foods and sounds of children chattering in excitement. The little bus frowned. Today was the day he had been preparing for as long as he could remember. But now that it was here, all he wanted to do was close his eyes and go back to sleep.

Today was the first day of school. For the first time, Yellow would pick up children and drive them to their school building—all by himself! He loved children and wanted to feel excited...but he did not.

Instead, his belly ached. His wheels felt out of balance. And he couldn't stop his windshield wipers from their nervous *swish-swish-swishing*, even though there wasn't a rain cloud in the sky.

"Yellow Bus," called his father, "it's time for breakfast!"
Yellow rolled out of his parking spot and over to the gas tank, taking a small sip.
"You'll need more than that to make it through the day," said his mother gently.
Yellow swished his windshield wipers back and forth, back and forth.
"My dear," said his mother, "what's the matter?"

Yellow didn't want to tell his parents how he felt, especially after they had worked
so hard to get him ready for this day. But he wondered if he could delay the day, at
least for a little while.

"My tires feel low on air," said Yellow. "Maybe I should wait until tomorrow to start."
His father circled around to check the tires. "They seem all right to me."
"I'm worried about my oil too," said Yellow. "It seems a little stale."
"It was just changed last week, darling," said his mother as she rolled up next to him.
"You are going to be amazing today."

But Yellow did not feel amazing. Whether or not he was ready, it sounded like today was going to be the day. He suddenly felt really scared. There were so many things that could happen while he was on the road, all alone, for the very first time. His windshield wipers swished faster and faster.

Swish-swish. Swish-swish. Yellow imagined stopping in front of a house. Instead of little children coming out to greet him, though, it was a herd of great big elephants!

They were stampeding toward him, and what could he do?!

Swish-swish. Swish-swish. Yellow imagined swerving down a

steep road with endless curves. At the bottom of the road was the

school, but he couldn't figure out where to go to drop the children off.

The children were going to be late, and it was all his fault!

School

Swish-swish. He imagined the kids refusing to board him, preferring to ride another bus and leaving him all alone with no one to ride with!

Swish-swish. He imagined even if he got to drop the children off at school, he might get lost and confused trying to find his way back to the road. What if he couldn't find his way home?

Yellow had turned a pale lemon color as he kept imagining all the awful things that could happen. Finally, he found his voice.

"What if...something really bad happens today?" he asked his mother and father.

"Yes," said his mother. "The world can be scary sometimes, but more often it can be wonderful. Your imagination is very powerful, and I wonder... What if something really *good* happens today?"

"You could meet a new friend," said his father. Yellow loved new friends.

"You could be washed clean by a sudden rain shower," said his mother. Yellow loved the rain.

"You know you'll be helping others," said his father. Yellow truly loved to help others.

Though the Little Yellow Bus heard his parents' words, he still couldn't make his mind imagine good things. He still had one worry that was just too big to imagine away…

"What if I just can't do this?" Yellow said. His wipers had stopped now, and his head was down. His headlights were dim. "It feels too big. I don't think I'm ready."

"Maybe you're not ready to tackle the whole day at once," said his mother. She parked in front of Little Yellow so they were bumper to bumper. "But I bet you're ready to start your engine. You do that every morning."

"Yes," said Yellow, "I suppose I can do that." His engine purred to life.

"And now that your engine is started, you might as well drive to the roundabout, like we practice every day," said his father.

"I guess I can do that too," said Yellow. He followed his parents as they maneuvered out of their lot.

As Yellow's wheels turned, his mind began to clear. He knew what do to next even without his parents saying so. He had to check his necessary systems—

lights,

wipers,

door,

horn.

Everything was in working condition.

Next, he had to make sure his seats were clean and clear. Yes, all was good there too. And it felt good to do these things on his own.

"Maybe," said Yellow, "I'll just do things one stop at a time."
"Yes!" said his father. "Now, remember to go…"
"Slow," said Yellow.
"Watch out for…"
"Bumps," said Yellow.
"And when in doubt…"
"Yield," said Yellow.

These were the things his father reminded him every day.
Saying them now comforted Yellow.

"And don't forget," said his mother "It's OK to be a little nervous when trying something new. And if you feel a little scared or worried today, just take a moment and remember—no matter how near or far apart, we're always there inside your heart." Mother gently tapped his hood and continued, "Every time you stop at a stoplight, you can imagine your father and I on either side of you, like we've practiced so many times. Your journey is just beginning, my love, and we know you can do this."

"I can try," Yellow said.

Yellow shifted from park to drive, and his wheels began to roll again.

Roll-roll. Roll-roll. Yellow imagined making a new friend. Maybe it would be a crossing guard or a child. Maybe it would be another bus!

Roll-roll. Roll-roll. Yellow imagined a rain shower. The water splished and splashed on his roof and hood, clearing off dirt and making his yellow paint shine.

Roll-roll. Roll-roll. Yellow imagined helping the children get to school. He pictured happy faces as he dropped them off for a day of learning.

Yellow smiled as he imagined all these good things, waiting just around the corner. Excited and full of hope, he decided it was time to trust and make the turn.

"I think that I can do this," he said. And then he did!

When Yellow picked up the first child, a little girl with wide eyes and a green backpack, he noticed she looked nervous. Yellow opened his doors and patiently waited, but she hesitated to step up.

"It's okay," said the Little Yellow Bus. "Just imagine how great today could be!"

The little girl smiled and imagined. Today *could* be pretty great! Yellow honked his horn. *Toot-toot.* With a laugh, she joined Yellow on the bus.

Then another child got on, then another, and another, until all his seats were full. Yellow went slowly. He watched for bumps. And when in doubt, he yielded.

At every stoplight, he imagined his mother and father beside him, cheering him on, going through his day with him.

Yellow realized nothing bad happened. There were no giant elephants, he didn't get lost, and every child got on to go to school.

And even better, he had fun! The world didn't feel scary. It felt friendly and full of possibility, as wonderful as his parents had promised.

Before long, Yellow's seats were empty again. He had delivered every child to school, safely and on time—all by himself! The journey had gone so quickly, he'd barely had time to worry.

"Now I know I can do this," Yellow said, swelling with pride.

"And if I can do this," said Yellow,
"I wonder what else I can do!"